Grouchy
Uncle Otto

Grouchy Uncle Otto

by Alice Bach

Pictures by Steven Kellogg

Harper and Row, Publishers
New York, Hagerstown, San Francisco, London

GROUCHY UNCLE OTTO
Text copyright © 1977 by Alice Hendricks Bach
Illustrations copyright © 1977 by Steven Kellogg

FIRST EDITION

Library of Congress Cataloging in Publication Data
Bach, Alice.
  Grouchy Uncle Otto.

  SUMMARY: Oliver the bear goes to care for his sick,
grouchy uncle and finds he really can do some things
better than his smart twin Ronald.
  [1. Twins—Fiction. 2. Bears—Fiction] I. Kellogg, Steven.
II. Title.
PZ7.B1314Gr   [E]   76-24304
ISBN 0-06-020344-7
ISBN 0-06-020345-5 lib. bdg.

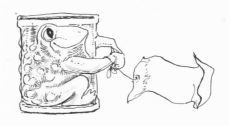

For Sarah Babb, a writer bear
and
For Ann Schumacher, a rare bear

"Since you are so smart, spell *thunderstorm*."

"That's a snap." Ronald stuck his nose in the air.

"Backwards, spell it backwards." Oliver laughed.

"You are so stupid. A gooseberry bush is a genius when you're around."

Oliver leaned over to punch Ronald's arm.

"Ronald, Oliver, I want to see you," Ma shouted out the door.

"Give me back my colored chalks," Ronald shouted.

"Indian giver."

"Bears, you have one minute to get in here."

Oliver landed a final punch.

Ronald ran toward the house. "Ma, he ripped my kite."

"He said I'm stupid." Oliver pushed Ronald aside and gripped Ma's paw.

"He is stupid," Ronald screamed as loud as he could.

Pa lifted Ronald onto his shoulder. "Ronald, I don't want to hear *stupid* again."

"Tell him, not me. He's the moron." Ronald's stumpy legs beat the air. His lips formed *stupid* over and over again—but he covered his mouth with his paw.

"Oliver, you are an all-around A-1 bear," Pa said, setting Ronald down on the floor.

"I'm an A-1 bear," Oliver repeated with an ice-cream look on his face.

"Uncle Otto has broken his arm and needs someone to take care of him. Think you can handle him, Oliver?"

Oliver shook his head. "He hates me. Last time he was here he said only pandas succeed at being cute and I'd better learn how to *do* something."

"I can read, write, and care for small animals, and I know all the names of places in the atlas," said Ronald. "You'd better learn something besides tearing other people's kites and whining to Ma. Isn't that right, Pa?"

"Ronald, you sound as mean as Uncle Otto. Don't worry, Oliver. When I was a cub, he said I looked too feeble to survive one winter."

"You, Pa?" Both Ronald and Oliver were amazed.

"It's hard for me to picture you as a cub because you're so big." Oliver sat on the floor and looked up at him.

"Even a puppy looks big if you lie on the floor." Ronald climbed on the table. "Now Pa looks small."

"Get off my clean table," Ma said.

"Oliver, Uncle Otto needs help. I know he has a gloomy streak, but do you think you can cook his food, tidy up his cabin?"

"Yes, Pa. I don't care how crabby he gets."

"We're very proud of you, Oliver." Ma and Pa waved good-bye.

"Come get me when you get stuck," Ronald called.

"I won't call you until all the honey in the world dries up."

Oliver ran into the woods and came out at Uncle Otto's cabin just as night turned the trees into black brooms sweeping a silver sky. He tapped lightly on the door.

"Stop that banging. You'll punch a hole in my door."

"Hello, Uncle Otto. I'm here to take care of you."

"I can see that you are here. Nothing wrong with my eyes." He sighed, pushed a mound of pillows onto the floor. "Which one are you?"

"I'm Oliver. Does your arm hurt a lot?"

"The arm, and my eyes sting, my legs ache, and my back feels twisted like ribbon candy."

"Does anything not hurt?" Oliver kept smiling, but inside he was moaning.

"I am one sick bear." Uncle Otto pulled up his quilt.

Oliver bent down and puffed the pillows. They were so large he could lift them only one at a time. "These pillows will make you feel better." Oliver panted as he heaved each pillow onto the bed.

"Better than what?" Uncle Otto snarled.

"Better than hot." Oliver laughed at his own rhyme.

"Don't get cute, Oliver. I can always rewrite my will. I don't have to give you so much as an acorn." He dipped his good paw into a washtub filled with gumdrops.

"What's a will?"

"A will, you foolish cub, is a formal document stating which bear is to receive what after I die. Your mother gets my copper watering can—if I don't get mad at her. Aunt Bear wants my string hammock. She's clever. It's the roomiest hammock in the woods. So far, she gets it. But I can change my will in a minute."

"I thought you just broke your arm." Oliver crammed his mouth full of gumdrops.

"That's all you can see. But an old bear, a very old bear, has a lot wrong inside too." He patted his stomach and shook his head. "Everybody dies—but few are smart enough to make a will." He coughed and wiped his eyes.

"Would you like a pot of tea, Uncle Otto?" Oliver wished he had magic eyes to see all the moldy parts wrong inside Uncle Otto.

"Tea might help." He groaned so loud Oliver stepped back. "But I'm too weak to nibble more than a few of those chocolate-chip cookies your mother brought yesterday. She carried on about how wonderful my watering can was. I caught on right away that she came because she wants my watering can."

"But Uncle Otto, she has a copper watering can. I think she was being nice because you're sick. When I'm sick she doesn't yell. Even the time I threw up all over the floor after I ate a whole honeycomb." Oliver picked up the teapot. "These painted violets are beautiful. It's the nicest pot I've ever seen. What's this tag?"

"Everything has a tag—that's how I keep track of who should get what."

"I don't like thinking you're going to die."

"I have no intention of dying now or soon—although if you don't give me those cookies and put two more spoons of sugar in my tea, I might melt away from hunger." Uncle Otto flipped over so his broken arm rested on a pile of pillows. He groaned and mumbled something that Oliver couldn't understand.

"The sugar bowl is pretty."

"Forget it. The whole set is promised," Uncle Otto said. He jotted something on the pad he always kept with him, shook his head, tore off the page, crumpled it, and tossed it on the floor.

"Are all these pages your will?"

"Burn them all. I'm making a lot of changes."

"You look healthy. I don't think you need to finish your will today."

"Don't count on my leaving you the tea set. It's one of my prize possessions. Everyone wants it." Uncle Otto shook his paw in Oliver's face.

"I don't want the tea set," Oliver said. He's even nastier than Ronald. Oliver unrolled a quilt. "If you need anything, call me." He nestled into the quilt. "I'm one tired bear."

"When you get old as I am, you won't be able to sleep. I never sleep," Uncle Otto said. And before Oliver could stick out his tongue at the old grouch, he heard Uncle Otto's ear-splitting snores.

Oliver woke up when something tickled his face. He opened his eyes and water splashed into them. He rolled over and wiped his wet face on the quilt.

"Uncle Otto! Stop."

"It's hard to wash with one arm in a cast. Nobody helps me."

"I'll help you." Oliver gritted his teeth. He did not want to fail Ma and Pa. If being an A-1 bear meant being kind to Uncle Otto, who was worse than a nest of hornets, well he'd be kind, kind, kind.

"I'm hungry as a weak bear can be. Maybe a few pancakes with syrup and some muffins." He pushed a pile of books onto the floor.

"Of course." Oliver was going to be the sweetest syrup, thicker than honey. He mixed pancake batter, then searched for some berries. As he opened each cupboard, he noticed every cup, platter, and spoon had a tag with someone's name on it. "Where are the berries, Uncle Otto?"

"There are no berries until you pick them. Didn't your mother teach you how to bake?"

"Yes, but I thought—" He went back to the cupboard to see if any of the tags said *Oliver*.

As soon as breakfast was ready, Uncle Otto sneezed so hard the tea sloshed onto the table. "Be careful, you've spilled my tea," Uncle Otto shouted, so loud a pile of logs next to the fireplace rolled into the center of the room.

Oliver squeezed his paws. Why should he have to take so much meanness? Why didn't Ronald get a dose?

"Where's my food?" Uncle Otto was whining.

"Do you want to eat on a tray in bed?"

"Certainly. I'm too weary to sit on a hard chair."

"I'd like to pour tea on your head," Oliver muttered.

"If I don't get some water, I'll choke."

Oliver reached for a mug. It was shaped like a frog whose front legs made the handles. Its tag read *Oliver*. He tingled. He loved that lime-green frog with its brown china bumps. He filled it with water and carried it to the bed.

"Be careful, it's not your frog yet." Uncle Otto's large paw clawed at the air. He struck the mug. They both stared at the shattered pieces on the floor.

"It's not my frog *ever*," Oliver said, brushing tears off his cheek.

"Sweep up the pieces or I'll cut my poor old feet."

I'd like to sweep the sharpest pieces into your bed, Oliver grumbled to himself. "Yes, Uncle Otto," he said. Being an A-1 bear was not an easy job. Let Ronald be an A-1 bear. He can have all the tags. I'd rather play in the woods.

"My arm aches inside this cast. I can't rub it. My feet are twitching. There's a draft on my neck. It's an old cabin, leaky and useless. Just like me. Nobody cares about an old bear."

"If Ma and Pa didn't care, they wouldn't have sent me."

"I have a high fever. I need another quilt. Who is rustling at my door?"

"Good morning!" Ma set down her basket. "Apple?"

Uncle Otto groaned and Oliver reached for the apple.

"Pear?" she said, smoothing the covers.

Uncle Otto groaned and Oliver reached for the pear.

Ma took the teapot to the sink, zigzagging around the piles of books.

"Teapot's promised," Oliver said softly.

"What did you say?" Ma asked.

"Look at the tag; it means who gets his teapot," Oliver explained.

"Oh, pooh, Uncle Otto's been doing that tag nonsense since I was smaller than you."

"He isn't going to die?"

"Of course he's going to die, but not from a broken arm. He thinks nobody likes him."

"That's a fact," Oliver said.

"Shh. He thinks people will like him if he promises them things, like his teapot, his frog mug."

"It broke this morning, and it was going to *me*." Oliver stamped his foot.

"He will change his tags ten times ten before he dies."

"Ronald will be that way too."

"Only Ronald?" Ma smiled.

"I never take back anything till Ronald does first. Then I have to or he would have everything."

"My eyes are burning as though someone set a match to them."

"Poor Uncle Otto, you seem very sick," Ma said as she put a cloth on his forehead. "Too sick to read, aren't you?"

"Not that sick. I'm not dead, I can still change my will."

"Of course you can." Ma sounded like she was talking to one of her cubs. "You'll have to take one tag off this clock," she whispered and winked at Oliver.

"My feet are like ice, I need another pillow, my back is stiff as though I had carried a cord of wood."

"Here's a pillow, Uncle Frogmug." Oliver gasped and buried his face in the pillow.

Ma winked at Oliver and he felt better. "I'll collect wood, Ma." Oliver backed out the door, relieved to be out of the house. He bumped into Ronald.

"Too much for you, huh?"

Oliver started to explain. Then he stopped. "Ma said if you showed up I should tell you to gather wood behind the house."

"Even Ma knew you couldn't handle a sick old bear. Too bad, but don't worry, I'll always take care of you, even when we're old."

"Making me do all the rotten jobs, right?" said Oliver as Ronald disappeared behind the house.

"Oliver, come here, dear." Ma was tying her bonnet. "I've left food for lunch and dinner. Pa will be over this afternoon." She leaned down to kiss him. "Cheer up, you're doing an A-1 job."

"I'll gather berries, Uncle Otto. Call me if you need anything. Maybe you can nap."

"How can I nap?" he snapped. He was snoring before Oliver picked up the berry basket and went outside.

Ronald was reading a large book with no pictures. Oliver shook the book. "Only a smart bear, the very smartest, could deal with Uncle Otto. Since he would be furious if we switched, why don't you say you're me?"

"Sounds dumb to me, but he needs me." Ronald tugged on his ear and ran toward the house. "Maybe I can convince him to tag all the books *Ronald*." He hugged himself in joy.

"I'll be out here if you can't take it," Oliver called. "Good luck, *Oliver*." He lay down on the grass and chuckled.

"What's all the banging and slamming? Oliver, I need some water, and my feet are icy again. What's for lunch?"

"Here's a cool pillow, Uncle." Ronald struggled with the large pillow.

"You sound peculiar."

Ronald laughed. This masquerade was going to be more fun than he had imagined. By the time he went home, Uncle Otto would think Oliver was the dumbest bear in the woods. "More tea, Uncle?"

"Yes, Oliver. And a back rub."

"OK, turn over on your stomach." Ronald picked up a log. "Rub-a-dub-dub," he sang as he scratched his uncle's back.

"Oliver, what are you doing? Put that log down. You'll give me a back full of splinters."

"Sorry. If Ronald were here, he'd know how to rub your back. Ronald knows everything."

"He's a snooty bear. Takes after his father. Never did care for that branch of the family. Where's my tea?"

"Want sugar in it?"

"Of course, two spoons. What's wrong with you?"

"I have a bad memory." He picked up a mixing spoon and shoveled sugar into the cup.

"Not that much sugar. I'll turn into a candy bear. You are not going to kill me to get at my tea set."

"I don't want anything, Uncle. But Ronald should get the globe, because he knows everything about geography. He can tell you the capital of any place."

"Then he doesn't need a globe. By the way, where is your lazy brother?"

"Lying in the sun doing what he's best at— thinking. He's the first one up each morning. Why? Thinking. Last one asleep each night. Why? Thinking."

"Sounds to me like a small bear's brain would get sore from so much thinking."

The kettle whistled and Ronald moved toward the stove. "OK, Uncle, tea and a few of these muffins?"

"Just a few. My appetite is smaller than a hummingbird's egg."

Ronald noticed Oliver listening outside the window. He hissed, "What was your problem? He's a snap to please."

"Oliver, what's all the whispering? I want hot tea, if anybody cares."

"Here you are, Uncle. You look a little better. You're lucky Ronald taught me everything I know about caring for sick bears." He'd have the books before sunset.

"Did he?"

Ronald nodded.

"He taught you to cook?"

"Of course. I don't read recipes very well. Ronald has all the delicious ones memorized."

"He taught you to build a fire?"

"Yes, and how to puff pillows their plumpest. How to adjust the curtains so the sun comes in every place in the cabin except in your eyes. Ronald could benefit from having this entire cabin all to himself. He would make it a permanent bear library. Maybe you'd like to chat with Ronald? He could drop by this afternoon."

THE GREAT ROMP

HOARDING HONEY

BEEZLEY

"Ronald sounds very smart." Uncle Otto yawned and then called, "Come in here, Bear under the window."

Oliver came in carrying his berry basket. "I'm sorry, Uncle Otto. I couldn't take care of you. I thought since Ronald is so smart—"

"Ronald isn't so smart. He's kept all the nasty traits he always had. Hand me those tags, Oliver. Can you spell globe?"

"*G-l-o-w-b?*"

"No. You'd better brush up on your spelling." Uncle Otto wrote something on a tag and attached it to the globe. Ronald was edging toward the door. He hoped he could sneak out unseen.

"Come back here, Smart Bear."

"Uncle, I was only playing around. I didn't mean it."

"If you don't watch yourself, you'll end up grouchy as your Uncle Otto. I was the smartest bear when I was a cub. No other bear could match me. Certainly not you. But smart grew into snappish, a first cousin to mean. And you're not smart enough or mean enough to be competition for me. Do you know how many bees to a hive?"

Ronald shook his head.

"How many clouds in the sky?"

Ronald shook his head.

"I am still the smartest bear." Uncle Otto leaped out of bed.

A tear ran down Ronald's cheek. Oliver danced around in a little circle. "Uncle Otto, no one ever said he was smarter than Ronald."

"Just so you don't forget about the bad side of smart, I'm going to rewrite my will and turn my cabin into a library for all the bears in this wood."

"Can I stamp all the books and tell all the bears where to find what they are looking for?" Ronald looked excited again.

"You'll have to ask the head of the library. What do you say, Oliver?"

"I'll have to think it over." Oliver smiled smugly.